THE SOUP STONE

Retold and Illustrated by

Iris VanRynbach

Greenwillow Books, New York

Pen-line and watercolors were used for the
full-color art. The text type is Della Robbia.

Printed in Hong Kong by South China Printing Co.
First Edition   10 9 8 7 6 5 4 3 2 1

Library of Congress Cataloging-in-Publication Data

VanRynbach, Iris   The soup stone.
Summary. When a family claims it has no
food to feed him, a hungry soldier proceeds
to make a soup with a stone and water.
[1. Folklore—France] I. Title.
PZ8.1.V36 1988   398.2'1'0944   [E]
86-31830   ISBN 0-688-07254-2
ISBN 0-688-07255-0 (lib. bdg.)

FOR MY PARENTS AND MICHAEL

There was once a soldier who was on his way home from the war. The distance between villages was great, and he had little hope of finding shelter before the night set in.

But at last he came to a farmhouse
on the outskirts of a village.

The soldier stopped at the house and asked the
farmer for shelter and something to eat.
"I'm sorry, but what with the war and the poor harvest,
we have little food to spare," replied the farmer.
"Have you got a large pot and water to fill it?"
asked the soldier.
"Yes, of course," replied the farmer.
"I have a soup stone with me," said the soldier.
"A soup stone, what is that?" asked the farmer.
"Fill the pot with water and put it on the fire, and
I will show you," replied the soldier.

When the farmer's wife had filled the pot, the soldier said, "This is a recipe cherished by my family."

He took the stone out of his pocket, turned it three times, and tossed it into the pot.

The soldier stoked the fire and the whole
family gathered around to watch.
"This will be a good soup," he said, "but some
salt would help the flavor. Could you spare
a bit of salt?"
"Of course," said the farmer's wife.
She took the salt box out of the cupboard,
and the soldier took a fistful of salt and threw
it in the pot.

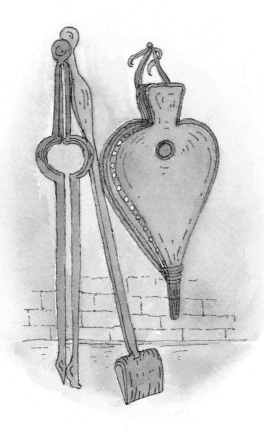

"I've used this soup stone so many times, the soup may be rather thin. You wouldn't have a carrot or two, would you?" asked the soldier.

The farmer's wife told the oldest daughter to run out to the garden and pull up a few carrots. The carrots were cleaned, and into the pot they went. While the soup boiled, the soldier told them about his adventures.

"If only we had a handful of potatoes, this soup would be just right," the soldier said. "But we have all learned to do without, so it's no use thinking more about it." The soldier stirred the soup.
"Well, I do think we have a few potatoes in the root cellar," said the farmer's wife. "I'll run out and have a look." Back she came with a handful of potatoes and some salted beef, and into the pot they went.

"What a grand soup it will be," they all agreed.
"Good enough for the best in the land, and all from
a stone."
"If only we had an onion and some cabbage, this
soup would be fit for a Christmas dinner," said the
soldier.
"Run down the road to the neighbors and ask if
they can spare an onion and a cabbage from their
garden," the farmer told his son.
The son did as he was told and before long came
back with a cabbage and a few onions. And into
the pot they went.

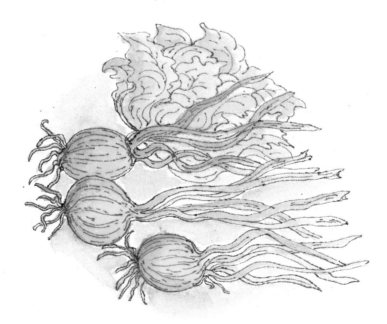

The soldier stirred the soup. "Mmmm, what a good smell!" They all sat down and talked about the war as the soup bubbled away.

"We must set a fine table for such a grand meal," said the farmer's wife. She took out their best plates and set a lovely table with flowers in the middle. A loaf of bread and some cider were brought out, and at last the soup was ready.

They all lined up with their bowls
while the farmer's wife served them
from the steaming pot.

Then they sat down to enjoy their meal.
"The best soup I've ever had," said the farmer.
"The tastiest I've ever eaten," said his wife.
They finished the soup down to the last drop.

After dinner they sat by the fire and sang songs
and told stories. The farmer's wife invited the
soldier to spend the night in the barn, sheltered
from the cold.

The next morning, when the soldier was ready to leave, he gave the soup stone to the farmer's wife. She protested, but he said, "I want you to have it. If you make the soup the way we did last night, the soup stone will never fail you."
The soup stone was put in a place of honor on the mantle.

"Such people don't come your way very often," said the farmer, as the family watched the soldier disappearing into the distance.

Luckily, the soldier hadn't gone very far before he found another soup stone, right in the middle of the road.